THE HALO OF DESIRE

By the same author

Poetry:

Umbrellas in the Snow

Translations:

Notebook of Shadows: Selected Poems of Philippe Denis (1974–1980)

Ask the Circle to Forgive You: Selected Poems of Nichita Stanescu (1964–1979) (with Mariana Carpinisan)

THE HALO OF DESIRE

Poems by
Mark Irwin

THE GALILEO PRESS LTD

Baltimore, Maryland

Published by The Galileo Press, Ltd., 15201 Wheeler Lane, Sparks, Maryland 21152

Typography by Capitol Communication Systems, Crofton, Maryland. Production by Joyce Kachergis Book Design & Production, Bynum, North Carolina.

Publication of this book was made possible in part by grants from the National Endowment for the Arts and from the Maryland State Arts Council.

This book has been typeset in Galliard.

Cover Art: "The Sistine Chapel: The Creation of Man," by Michelangelo. Reprinted with permission of the Vatican Museum.

LIBRARY OF CONGRESS
CATALOGING-IN-PUBLICATION DATA
Irwin, Mark.
    The halo of desire.
    I. Title.
PS3559.R95H35   1987   811.54   87-80090
ISBN 0-913123-12-9
ISBN 0-913123-13-7 (pbk.)

First Edition

For John Hobbs and Randi Schulman
For David

ACKNOWLEDGEMENTS

Grateful acknowledgement to the editors of the following periodicals in which many of these poems appeared:

Antaeus: "Dandelions," "The Distance of Flesh"
Antioch Review: "Augustifolia," "Integrity," "Rue Saint Denis"
Atlantic Monthly: "Vermeer"
Akros: "Poem for Edvard Munch"
Intro 11: "Narcissus," "Trees"
Malahat Review: "Stars and Trees"
Mid American Review: "The Gold Coin," "To a Fallen Starling"
The Nation: "The Creation of Man: The Sistine Chapel"
The Ohio Review: "Bucharest"
Poetry Now: "Wild Strawberries"
Quarry West: "Aubade"
Shenandoah: "The Invention of the Snowman"
Writing Poems (Little, Brown): "Icicles"

Several of these poems appeared in a limited edition, *Umbrellas in the Snow,* Bits Press, 1985, and are reprinted here by permission of the author.

"Things that divine us we never touch"

—Charles Wright

CONTENTS

THREE

FOUR

ONE

. . . Perhaps the blue color of water and ice is due to the light and air they contain, and the most transparent is the bluest. Ice is an interesting subject for contemplation . . . Why is it that a bucket of water soon becomes putrid, but frozen remains sweet forever? It is commonly said that this is the difference between the affections and the intellect.

–Thoreau

The Charm

The way you took your hand from your hip
as if to promise
me water
and I stood for a long time where
the waves broke
equaling out in sunlight
like your hair
that kept on falling
until it never reached your shoulders
and I was unsure
whether I should wait   or follow.

The Boy

loved coins. The grace
and simple weight
of money. Liberty
standing on a date, 1920,
clothed in silver flowing robes
with silver stars along her thighs.
Silver, silver, silver.

And all about the tiny sky
above her hair
a rainbow spread for years
in hues of tarnished gold
and copper

that slowly faded
and lost their sheen, the myth
exchanged for luck
that rode with other coins
forever in his pocket
until her face and body wore
featureless and plain,

yet the memory to his thumb
waxed more sure
from all that had become truth
and all that was
once beauty.

Dandelions

To see their heads
by low sun,
spheres that seem to rise
like tiny balloons, illumined
and buoyed with light,
is to understand their vacancy.

Watching them closely—
trying to decide
what color grows there,
frail as the curls
of cigarette smoke
around an old man's face,
or blurred
like the circular flick
of bicycle spokes
when a child pedals away.

As a boy, getting
on my hands and knees,
looking through the eye of one,
a camera's lens
out of focus.
The colors were the same—
like seeing glass through glass.

Now by moonlight,
moons themselves—
less bold though,

shy as a film's negative
waiting to be developed.

They cast no shadow.
Heads hold a faint glow
still allowing transparency.
One looks through seeds
at the thimble
from which they grow—
that which dies.

My thoughts rise
in the dark now
like the faint balloons
these dandelions once were.
They each carry
a small dream into night.
Morning will find them—
heads caved in with birth.

To a Fallen Starling

Haloed in gold, your lime eye
gone dull. Its slug remains in your once proud head
blinking grey beneath leaves
that twist in the glass-water light of evening.

How long since you slipped from the air
to limp, carrying
a load of flies on your back,
before I saw how fast

time was in the stalled present
where you slumped,
pulling your head to your breast,

crouching in that final glade
of heart-shaped leaves, where I, feather
to your breath, still approach.

Trees

Sometimes in my sleep
because I am never enough
in this world
as they are never enough
in their sky
I become a giant
searching any forest
to make a small
bouquet of them
and upon returning home
place them in a vase
for my son
who in his smaller sleep
will awake with me
and together
we will watch them
taking forever to go.

Vermeer

The piety of small joys.
Lace. Bread and
Milk. Faces bowed to letters
Or gentlemen
With visions of the world.
A laughing girl.

No more than this
Ever. Or all day
By a window
A woman weighing pearls.
God's equation
Of peace and light.

                                        —for Walter Strauss

9

Eve

Such perfect intuition is
a form to worship. You knew
then, the hell of unending, all

in an apple, so that paradise
was a kind of autumn;
yourselves, one with the present's

perfect drift. Better not to have
said a word to Adam
whose lips touched names upon the animals

while you dreamed of zoos, shepherds
dying. Not the green spaces
you would leave, but her awkward sister,

time. You knew that we as humans
were meant to swerve, to wake from sleep
and carry the knowledge of seasons on our tongues.

–for John Drury

Father

There are some roads that a son
never forgets. One lies just outside
Kingsport, Tennessee. It goes
back and forth between our house
and your car and I am on my knees
holding onto your leg as you drag me
to the black Fairlane's door and say
are you coming, or will you stay
with her? Father, wait, for although
we rehearsed it several times
I am still making up my mind
as the gravel and stones of our drive
slosh and scrape against my knees.
Do they not sound like the sea?
The long, slow tide of you going
out; mother, small, hunched by the door
saying please, please think of your son
as I hang by your coat, its cargo.
Father, how many tons did it weigh?

Wings

On the road to Cheia
just outside of Ploiesti
where the fields rise to the blue Carpathians
we stopped for half an hour while a train passed,

And Nichita spoke
of when he was a boy
and the American bombs fell like hornets from the sky
lighting up the steel derricks in plumes of flame and purple smoke,

Of how walking home from school
he saw a man wearing fire on his back
scream and roll, then print his shape in the dirt.

Together we left that car
and wandered far over the sere and cratered fields
to a hedgerow filled with the light chattering song of sparrows.

We watched them rise
in a flurried arc, then fall
to the ground where they scalloped
the dust, raising small clouds that held

In the sunlight
and flute end of their song
toward which we walked, slowly, then kneeled
to touch what faint print wings leave on the earth.

—for Nichita Stanescu

Domnica

I remember how she rose with nothing on
but water, as the pool's aqua mirror lapsed

and closed beneath her thighs
as she pulled up onto the chrome ladder

then stood, her dripping hair, dripping sunlight.
And though she stepped from, she never

really stepped from water, for she was made
of light and water. The blue chips of her eyes

shone clear, for like a child, there was nothing on her mind
but wonder, as she lay upon the grass

to dry, and I would marvel at her breasts
whose tips, a swollen shade of coral,

seemed forever slowed in blossom, while all the summer turned
about the flower of her thighs

whose taste was that of ash, and that of honey.
I say this with no regret, many autumns later.

Eurydice Talking

Sometimes we make it to the landing.
I do this for you, after
All, even agony prolonged
Becomes a joy,
And this is repetition.
The garish snapshot in your mind,

Why am I so patient?
When you place your hand
Upon the rail, I know my name
Rumors light like running water

As you stray between the yes and no
Then turn to flood the darkness.
What can I tell you?
Desire cannot be commanded.

Once is now, this undertow
Forever. Keep turning.
It was your carelessness
That makes the song worth singing.

Icicles

Slender beards of light
hang from the railing.

My son shows me
their array of sizes:

one oddly shaped,
its queer curve

a clear walrus tooth,
illumined, tinseled.

We watch crystal cones
against blue sky.

Suddenly some break loose,
an echo of piano notes.

The sun argues
ice to liquid.

Tiny buds of water
pendent on dropper tips

push to pear shapes,
prisms that shiver silver

in a slight wind
before falling.

Look, he says laughing,
a pinocchio nose,

and grabs one
in his small hand,

touching the clear carrot,
cold to his lips.

Narcissus

Idol boy so loved by all
you loved none

save the one
you could never have

pooled in a blue park
of sky and self.

If love was languor
you were both.

While others quested
you would rest

sleepless nights
leaning again with day

above a gaze so full
filled only with itself.

Piero Della Francesca:
The Victory of Heraclius Over Chosroes

Dressed like girls in fabulous pastels
they move into battle.
Everything is beautiful, the flanks
of the swan-white horse, its ass
over the dying man's face,

Or the blue dagger etching blood
on another's splayed neck.

Yet there is neither love nor hatred,
only the pure math of color.

The rose helmets and celadon shields
do not move
but rest like vases on a mantel,

Forever perfect,
forever glassy and shattered.

Proserpina

Proserpina, sleep.
The pass through hell
as that to love
is narrow.
Yet you will survive the dreams
and us
the wrack of checkered days.

Wake not by force,
but as you walk
reversed among his orchards,

Taste the pomegranate
whose skin is like a sun
for flowers lost on earth.

TWO

Hurry, hell is forever at hand,
which one cannot say of heaven.

> —The fool
> *RAN*, Akira Kurosawa

The Creation of Man: The Sistine Chapel

Then I remember being drawn toward him
as my mind snapped alive
like light cast back from water

And my face, flushed, lifted
like a flower petal's muscle

But my arm and wrist remained limp
like a stem without water

As my eyes teared in the choiring wind
that became his white, streaming
hair and beard

That framed the fierce gaze
that directed the finger
that said rise

rise from the mud in my likeness.

And I half-rose toward him
out of the earth's languor
because of this
and what lay half-hidden, peering
over his far shoulder.

Oh she looked at me afraid
but with desire
like I at him.
I knew this was woman,

And in my dream looked further

toward the joy   blue   green   future
where there was a garden

Whose gate
slammed shut forever

And my face nodded down
like a rose beyond summer, autumn
and a long, long winter

Until I felt my flesh smear
like mud anew
as the pastels, their
pigments in plaster set in

And with my tatooed eyes saw
another face
not looking down but upwards—
tired, paint-streaked and mortal.

And I loved this man strapped to the scaffold,
loved him as though he were my father.

The Distance of Flesh

is a sadness, yet still
I place this picture of you
in a scrapbook,
thumbing by chance to a photograph
of your father's just-wed parents.

Their faces shine like coins,
yet live only in memory
as does your father
whose death
left your mother half alive.

As kids we threw pennies in a pond
to see some kissing goldfish.
Their mouths seemed locked for hours.
So close, we could have dreamed them.
As close as loss itself.

Once I saw a man
set himself on fire.
His body lit in flames kept lifting up
as if to stand and walk away,
the tired hero of a film.

I say I'll forget
but I can't.
To forgo the love of flesh
one must be a saint.

I toss this scrapbook in the fire.
I can't look at photos.

The distance of flesh is a sadness,
the body's soul a doll on earth
passed from heir to heir.

Making a Woman

All winter
I have been making a woman
from twigs, sticks, and flowers.
I work slowly, for many times I have failed.
I work alone, ignoring my friends;
and of course, I can afford no lover.

For her legs I choose the stems
from two small saplings.
They are strong and well-tapered;
for a woman's legs, though sleek,
must be strong to carry a child
or to leave a man.

Working through March, I carve arms
from the smaller parts of those saplings.
And though I live in doubt
whether I can form a face
that will not embarrass her
                              I try

Carving from a mushroom's top
an almost perfect oval,
then contour with a knife the higher cheeks
and nose, impressions where the eyes will go
for which I choose two apple seeds.
Then lips, from that apple's skin,
I cut by memory with a razor.

As the weather grows more sure
I begin the final work:
for her hair I choose wisteria,
its vine turned auburn from last year's sun;

for hands I cut glove shapes from a lily;
and on the bottom of each leg
I attach a thorn so she might stand.

Last, I dress her in a blouse
made from a dahlia's petals—
then hang a makeshift skirt,
three amber leaves about her waist.

On the first cloudless day
I take her outside,
set her upright in the grass and sunlight.

And though the sun
makes a jewel of her lips
and stirs perhaps the sap in her legs,
she does not seem enough.

Already the body's begun to rot.
The face is a peel of dark,
the lips curl, losing their color.
A fly lands on one hand, tearing it off.

Now, seeing what a poor thing I have made,
I know that I must destroy her.
With a quick breath I rip her blouse.
With a match I light the leaves of her skirt,
then last, her hair, a flame
whose orange wing argues her up

With the first soft floatings of ash
like flowers.

July

The month not long begun
and everything approaches a stellar calm.
By night, high in the sky's black dome
                              Cygnus plunges south
through the Milky Way's long cloud.

Now the brightest stars
of the Eagle, Swan, and Lyre
compose an equilateral triangle
that slides away with the oncoming fall.

If you stay up late
you will see threaded meteors hang,
cluster, pop, and break
like mulberries on a hot summer's day.

And if you stay up till dawn
you will no longer hear
the impetuous spring songs of birds,
for they have raised or lost their young
and are reconciled, like you,
with things the way they are.

And if you look about your garage
you will see spider webs
spun fine, dangling in the humid air
the way the Milky Way dangles higher.

And if you look closer
you will see, as if spinning there
about the fat female spider

her tiny young circling like planets
thrown out by the conflagration of a star.

And if you walk out onto your lawn
you will see the roses
their spiralled petals blossomed out full
as if to accept some thing from above,

something weighted, cumbrous, and about to fall.
And if you keep walking
there is no end
for you have entered the middle of all things.

Integrity

I am troubled by the integrity of things,
this hand-blown vase given to you by another.
I fill it with wild flowers—
violets, milkweed, foxglove and fennel,
then place it on the window sill.
The wind blows the flowers
not the vase that breaks in three pieces.
What will you say? Will you smile
in anger, cry perhaps, twice surprised
at the bright flowers and broken glass?
I glue the vase and wonder at the whole.
Did he conceive its curved shape in three parts
after picking flowers, or making love to you?
I wonder if love is divisible by anger,
or the fear that forms its fragile bond?
It would take three hands to remake this vase.
Three hands to grasp its happenstance.
One to make, one to take, and one to break—
to circle and pass the pieces.

                              —for Mariana Carpinisan

31

The Gold Coin

The gold coin I bought as a boy
shines in my pocket.
The fine intaglio Indian
wears a headdress of feathers
worn smooth by the years.

Always in autumn I carry it
to slip in and out of my pocket
the way my father's father would his watch
to wind and worry away
hours of the Depression.
His vest held that ghost-like ticking,

and I used to think
that pulling the heavy gold braid
made it tick louder or faster
when together we would slip like sunlight
between the trees of that park
and I would ask him of Indians.

Now that man is gone
and because I fear
when green things bloom to a crimson
        I take that coin
and drop it in the park,

then pretend to be
the son of some other man
until I see that gold
flash the secret by which I am deceived—
what time designs upon us all
the slow intaglio of years.

Rue Saint Denis

There is a street in Paris called Saint Denis
full of bums and empty bottles
and always someone selling flowers,
where trees spread their green among the reds of whores.
Once, in spring, I bought flowers here,
three tulips from a toothless man
who wore this world in his eyes.
A mold, or stuff like snow, bloomed
in their blue, as clouds in the sky.
If there is a weather called love,
it is here, where a toothless man
smiles among whores for all he's worth.
His hands held tight on the stems of tulips
until someone tosses him a few francs.
Carrying those flowers to you, walking through
that carnival of spring and sex I thought—
green is the color that rusts our bodies
until our fortunes become like flowers.
When the petals fall, the sexual parts are left.

Achilles

Later, you spent
lovely Penthesileia
and to the horror of others
made love to the spoiled corpse.
What did you possibly think?
Not even can a god
beget with the dead.

Finistère*

At Arcachon he found a young whore,
broad shouldered with small breasts.
They lay all night, never said

a word. Next morning he walked the pier,
stared out at the pewter sea
where white caps leaped like gulls

come down to feed. By noon
he had grown hungry, too,
and stopped at a small Dutch café

where local sailors ate
oysters colored like the winter sky
beat silver by a hint of sun.

And what beauty was left
was left there on a bed of
escarole, where six rough stones

clicked on an azure plate.
He ate them all. And as the day's
first beam of sunlight

pierced the glass of Chardonnay,
he raised his head
a bit, and felt ashamed.

* Finistère is a coastal region in southwestern France which borders
  the Atlantic Ocean.

Poem for Edvard Munch

Between love's blush and death's pallor
is a short distance
so I take detours.
The red light of your hair
and a hell of jealousy
show me the way.
The heart's pulse and limp
and blue shawl of loneliness
when the moon was the only coin I had
to bear the fear of it.

The Poet at Nine

Saturday afternoons he would watch
How slowly she dressed, her anticipation
Becoming his fear, her enjoyment
All delay, while light pooled in tiny bottles
Shaded pale cinnamon, rose, and apricot.

Soon the sitter would arrive and, not
Long after, the handsome man he hated so
When for a moment, as she turned
To blow her child a kiss, the scent
Of her perfume mixed with his cologne.

To what smoke-filled bar would she belong?
Beneath what table cross and uncross her legs
While shuffling bracelets up her arms?
How many times lean forward to a match,
While hanging on his whiskey breath?

Bucharest

Never before could I hear the word so clearly,
America, while the gypsy carts
clacked down Calea Victoriei.

The vacant shops like evening. Everywhere
lines. Women slapping down five lei for sugar.
The meat trucks on Strada Doctor Lister.

Nights. Blue smoke and vodka,
the sunken eyes of poets.
The girl from Sibiu, whose name
I carried like a star on my lips.

Blond mosquitoes stinging my head
from dream, New York,
the yellow cabs gliding down Broadway.

And each morning the sun that would
rise, gathering blue-smocked children to school,
like the day's terrible shadow.

Archaeology

We have been digging for hours,
Slowly troweling the clay-red
Soil, hollowing out the darker circles
Where rotted fence posts were.
For two weeks, nothing; then

Steel tine scraping bone, its echo
And gullied sound. A show of white.
The skull like a sullen root
You trace with the pick, as though it
Were etching your hand in chalk.

With a sable brush you dust
The brow. It is thin, not thick. A female.
We flesh out the skull. A few loose
Teeth, corn-yellow seeds, their crowns
Slow frozen flowers. We work

Into evening, shallowing out
The clavicles and sternum, each rib
—like building a cage of air—
The length of both arms and shattered
Hands offer the splayed pelvis,

Its ghost ear, a lobe-petalled
Fungus, listening from earth.
The legs, femur and tibia perfectly
Intact, interred with the dusk
As we step back and gaze. We are

Volunteers, volunteered to touch
What shines like a splintered moon

Held in relief. The coin of ourselves,
Our future's past, we look down
To save and spend in a glance.

Toward the Museum at Auschwitz

As they were starved, after the fifth
day, they were asked to shed their clothes.
Lesser Giacomettis, all of them.
On the sixth day, they gave up
rings, necklaces, and eyeglasses.
The last of their personal possessions.
There was a time, I was told, when naked men
walked timidly, like boys, ashamed,
but these had been clothed
in nothing too long. No one
made it to the seventh; I am not
amazed, not at that, but at what
remains behind glass walls.
The same nauseous yellow light
that falls upon a bed, illumines this poem.

Moonrise

Now in the twilit blue, the half halo
Rises, waxing marvelously full,
Pushing its white vowel

Up through the trees,
Casting a fine chalk spray
Onto the branches and sooty limbs

That bristle the blanched jowls
With a thousand wicks
It is the doused

Candle of.
Now full up and done
It glides free like a swan

No longer veiled to show
Leprous, shadowy scars
Towed like clouds

Beneath fine opal.
Now, more ugly and small,
It climbs to its bald perch

To brood over a nest of stones.

Narcissus in Hell

These affections of the heart
He finally shrugs off.
Pardon him

For if it appears
That he has loved too much
It was merely to escape
The night's bad luck.

Never once
Did he see himself whole
But always divided in flame.

Did he prefer
Deferring paradise
With these milder hells? Yes, perhaps,

But by escaping the leisure
Of water, and staring
Into the tissued spirals
Of flame, he slowly transcended his desire

And abandoned hope,
And by abandoning hope
He discovered joy.

Umbrellas in the Snow

We wear our lives in a worn-out town,
Play our nocturnes and watch the stars.
Love lies above us, we cannot bear it,
We carry umbrellas in the snow.

Between life and art, we try to live,
But our only art is a life of anguish.
Kids amuse us, shadows soothe us.
The bright light hurts our eyes.

Some winter days, without desire,
We hold each other but seldom move.
Our children cry when we try to kiss.
The listless way we make love.

Trains and taxis between wives and lovers,
Planes and churches between countries and gods.
We travel a lot but never leave,
We carry umbrellas in the snow.

THREE

Exsultate, jubilate,
o vos animae beatae,
exsultate, jubilate,
dulcia cantica, cantica canendo . . .

—Mozart, K. 165

How Can I Begin To Tell You?

Outside my window
robins nest in the rotting pear tree.
How can I begin to tell you
how the mating female
waits for the male
by fleeing him
until their wings, a double fluttering cross,
steady the air to conceive.

How can I begin to tell you
how over and over
she hollows the nest out,
the puffed arc of her breast
turning the half-sphere,
a capitol of desire.

How can I begin to tell you
about the male?
How the head will tilt
like a tiny weight
as the insect-eye
measures the air for food.

How can I begin to tell you
about the clouds, gathering, huge,
as the sunlight fails
into the violet air
and the small
treasure of eggs appears.

Stars and Trees

My son draws stars and trees
the trees always reaching far
for the stars just out of reach.

My son draws stars and trees,
my son one day will be a man
a man who will watch the stars

while his son sleeps in the night,
a son who during the day
will climb trees thinking of stars.

My son draws stars and trees,
and what do I have to tell
him who makes such simple poems.

Butterflies

Drams of color in the random sky.
There is no field enough
for wings halving the blue
air, or alight on any flower.
Not the bee's
crumbling strength, but the simple
one, two, threes of touch.

Forever in a minute's season
the sun's small fire through shade,
like your eye in mine—
or the more though never quite
tactile lashes on a sleeper's cheek.

Romanian Family Digging Potatoes

Just a family, three,
who in the rich, coffee-shaded earth,
stoop, digging them up, except the girl
off to one side, face poised
in the piecemeal light.

Her cheeks are rose
smeared with dirt. One
curl, the color of soil, falls
alongside her mouth. Her apron is full
and her lips verging on smile
as she looks down upon them,
fruit in a still life.

Love Poem

Because the coral tips of your breasts
are a shade more lovely
than the finest sun-bleached rose of any fresco,
I will touch the brush of my tongue upon them.

Because your skin
sheds a light more delicate than opals,
I will enter the dusk of your sleep
and lay my shadow on it.

Because the slow rise of your hips
remind me of the small hills
upon which as a child I stumbled
now I will fall upon them,

And like a rainbow
arch the prismed height of my desire
over the small cross of your body,
for only there can I observe you safely.

Mayflies

In the adult stage, they live only hours
or a few days, but the aquatic larval stage
may last for several years.

As though evening drew their delicate selves from water,

they rise, already old, nymphs
riding a bubble of air
to issue the wings in a paper murmur.
Elegant and lace-veined
they unfold,
inventing wind to join their thousands.

Now in air, they moult again
as though perfection had its flaws
before the body
—sleek and glistening—
can join the nuptial flight.

How many males
in a whirling rise and fall
tinsel the air, rainbow-hued,
until a female
borne upwards from below
will rise to conceive?

Aurelius, dying—said,
"Contemplate the nature of all things through change."
Yet what thing in nature
conjures life so short

that in its perfect, final state
should live but hours?

As these, gliding in twilight,
arc their threaded tails,
fountains of seeming endless repetition.

The females whirl, drift, mate
and drop their tiny mass of eggs
to rise beyond philosophies of dance
   —faint, bare fluttering—
      and fall, after.

The Perfectness

The perfectness of what
we do not know.

The tiny wisdom of first sight,
its touching glance.
A boy bent above a globe.

The perfectness of what
we do not know.

Wild Strawberries

Such chance is love
and us wandering this road
finding a field filled with them.

Our hands burn in a fever
the shy color of embarrassment.
So unsure is the sky above

that we pick faster
filling our shirts and hearts,
hoping to have enough to preserve

what's wild and never lasts.

Spring

How long will the forsythia's wicks of yellow phosphor
burn? I don't know
but the ants are building tiny volcanoes
between the sidewalk's cracks

As the iris slowly unfolds
four lavender flags
and my girl pulls her hair back in braids
to keep her forehead cool.

There are Times

when I reach
for a woman with no body,
and the reaching
is not so much to touch
but in praise
of having done so.
Art is loss,
the never wholly looking back
but ever turning
gesture of conceiving.

Shining with an Evenness
We Used to Call
Grace

To belong to no place,
and to belong to no person,
and not to be in love

is perhaps the beginning
of freedom,
and perhaps the beginning
of the knowledge
of self,

the great darkness
where the spark breeds
in the limitless straw
of space,

where the light, like that of a star
slowly gathering from cloud,

shines with an evenness
we used to call
grace.

Botticelli found it
in the taut young breasts of a girl
whose opal skin, still sea-wet,
seemed freshly unwound from a shell.

For he desired not the girl,
but the spring within the girl,

or tucked and concealed
between her beautiful thighs
the birthscent of creation
which is the birthscent of the sea.

FOUR

As from the earth the light Balloon
Asks nothing but release—

                    —Emily Dickinson
                    # 1630

The Invention of the Snowman

Somewhere beyond the bounds of sleep
my bones undressed, rising from their flesh
to become this selfless, falling dust.

It was then I wanted ears
with which to hear the familiar cries
of those children building me.

And of course I had no eyes
only this unfailing bandage of light,
the snow sewing its colorless view.

But worst of all, this thirst to be living—
to understand those small, clumsy hands
making the same careless mistakes as gods.

Augustifolia

When you see on a woman's face
a bruise, pale flotsam and purpling,
you may understand the orchid –
How at first one turns away from the vulgar
only to be stricken by beauty,
for the bruise of the flesh
is moving inward.

But when the dead come to live
having slipped so many times from your heart
there will be no more healing,
for the spirit
impossibly bruised will flower
everywhere at once,
almost more weed than flower –
like lavender or augustifolia.

And this color will become the flag of a country
as personal as a sadness,
yet generous as silence or water
from which others must finally drink to listen –
And the joy will come
so far from the other side
that you will hear the sunlight on
the rust from the rain through the bells.

The Salmon

Through green rivers necklaced with falls
they move beneath maples
flushing to scarlet
while the apples ripen, and grapes arrive
at their wreckage of purple.

Beneath the sun
red-embered and bloodshot,
they move with hooked jaw and humped back

to where they were spawned,
as though instinct were the memory of lust,
of survival passed on.

La Vita Nuova

Not the pastor's face in sunlight
or cool touch of his hand,
but having watched the men
in white smocks, the single-filed

cattle, the blade
in their throats and the groan
you don't hear through the glass.
Not the arrival, but return.

Your hands on the white sink
basin, your knees buckling like a girl's,
the rush of vomit that leaves

you clean and dizzy.
And the knowledge on the cool floor
that for you it is over.

Sun at Winter Solstice

On the horizon the gold clot darkens,
its molten glow like a memory
of having once been dross
while I, rocking back and forth,

bowing and nodding my head,
touching my cheek to the window,
gaze out through the glass beyond pines
where the blue dome of cold fades to rose.

How our blood smells and gleams of the earth,
how the earth shines like the guts of a star
and I stare at the copper pod

until the seed sparks fill my eyes
and I look down without regret
at the gold mask in my hands.

Church

And when all that is real
collapses, does God
shimmer on the wall like light
from a window
beautiful and insubstantial,
the limpid cameo
we touch to our cheek
as the dream
smears to precision,
the sound of stained glass
shattering, which only the mad
hear as bells?

The Distance

Can the distance between a man
and a woman be closed in a life?
The face of the man
finally become the glow of unconcern
while she takes on the worried brow.

Sleepwalkers who in fifty years
walk through one another.

All night
that moth flying against the bulb
is a moment,
yet in minutes I have seen
lovers drift apart like continents.

I think of the dream
in which I grow too fast to move.
The thought of raising a finger
forgotten in the length of an arm.
Movement itself a kind of immobility.

To know that rock is a slow forever,
the bird in flight a perfect center.

Aubade

We watch the geese fly over.
How effortlessly they cast
desire toward the open.
Soon they are miles away

Leaving us with autumn,
our less than perfect speech
and a few late bees
that trophy our flesh for warmth.

We sit in the museum park
and watch the swans
arc their lovely heads in water
to stall from kissing

Until desire casts us out,
our lips moving ahead of thought,
as though by living beyond ourselves
we touch.

Small Kingdoms

Not the dog's
coral pink intestines
splayed between asphalt and

gravel. He had long since
learned to look
away, but

the fluff of hair
that strayed from an early
May thistle. Blond blooming briefly

from purple,
until robbed by the Jay
and brought high to her nest

in an elm.
How quickly small
kingdoms are undone.

Patina

Beauty appears like silver; proof-
lustre where we see ourselves approach.
What we desire is the light thrown back.
Love, the glare of falling.
Trees in April after rain,
their green lips diamonded and wet.

Yet habit tugs us back.
Memory, that casual walk
among hills, the drowse of opal light
through watercolor maples
saying *come back*. As though safety were all patina.

Art

All my life
I have been drawn by its scent,
like that of an October orchard
which guides the young boy
until he stands
mesmerized before the pendulous red fruit
that hang in the cidered air.

And though the scent
grows stronger, still I am wandering,
afraid that when I finally arrive
I will merely discover
what is called life

where people occasionally
speak of a fleeting, yet exotic scent
called art, and a strange, but small
and seemingly purposeless
wandering tribe.

The Democracy of Love

Because we climbed so high
now this need to betray,
as though we might have
lost ourselves to perfection.

Were we afraid perhaps
that virtue is the end of will?
I think hell
is the dizziness of freedom.

Is it not the heart
which accuses, and humility
that is born from humiliation?

The Resurrection of Desire

As after rain when steel grey clouds
Part, the sudden buoyant light
From pools, small, shallowing
Like our patience gone, that call us out.

The Halo of Desire

In the blue lamp of evening
the face of a boy,

his cheeks touched with the rose color
of one cloud

at just that hour
when the sky is pale with stars.

You are learning the intelligence of dying

(suddenly aware
of the constellations that begin to appear,

great heroes, animals, and hunters
that wheel their braille
and fiery truths above

as if eternity
were something tactile)

and you have no other choice
than to become a child

to hold it
forgetfully in your arms.

Photo by William Johnson

Mark Irwin was born in Faribault, Minnesota, in 1953. He
has lived throughout the United States and abroad in France
and Italy. He has taught at the University of Iowa, the
Cleveland Institute of Art, and Case Western Reserve
University. Recently, he was a Fulbright lecturer at the
University of Bucharest, Romania. In 1984 he won a *Discovery
Award,* sponsored by the Poetry Center of the New York
YM-YWHA and *The Nation.*

ACQ3215

2/9/94
gift

PS
3559
R95
H35
1987